if i had a DRAGON
si yo tuviera un DRAGÓN

Written and illustrated by Tom & Amanda Ellery

Escrito e ilustrado por Tom & Amanda Ellery

Spanish translation by / Traducido al español por Teresa Mlawer

LECTORUM
PUBLICATIONS INC.
a subsidiary of Scholastic Inc.
New York

To our parents, who inspired us when we were young, and to our three Mortons—Tommy, Johnny, and Katie—who inspire us today.

And to Alisha Niehaus and Daniel Roode—for making it happen.

A nuestros padres, quienes nos inspiraron cuando éramos pequeños, y a nuestros tres Mortons, Tommy, Johnny y Katie, quienes nos inspiran hoy.

Y a Alisha Niehaus y a Daniel Roode por hacerlo realidad.

IF I HAD A DRAGON / SI YO TUVIERA UN DRAGÓN

Bilingual edition copyright © 2006 by Lectorum Publications, Inc.

Originally published in English under the title IF I HAD A DRAGON

Copyright © 2006 by Tom and Amanda Ellery

Published by arrangement with Simon & Schuster Books for Young Readers.

an imprint of Simon & Schuster Children's Publishing Division, New York

MORTON! PLAY WITH YOUR BROTHER!

¡MORTON, JUEGA CON TU HERMANO!

I don't want to play with my brother!
He's too little.

¡No quiero jugar con mi hermano!
Es muy pequeño.

I wish he would turn into
something fun. . .

Ojalá se convirtiera en algo
divertido. . .

…like a new kite,

…como un papalote nuevo,

or a bulldozer, or. . .

o una excavadora o. . .

...a DRAGON!
...¡un DRAGÓN!

If I had a dragon, I would be so happy.
We could go for walks...

Si yo tuviera un dragón, sería tan feliz.
Podríamos ir de paseo...

We could play basketball!

¡Podríamos jugar al baloncesto!

YOUR DINNER IS READY!

¡LA CENA ESTÁ LISTA!

Oh.

Ah.

Go for a swim?

¿Ir a nadar?

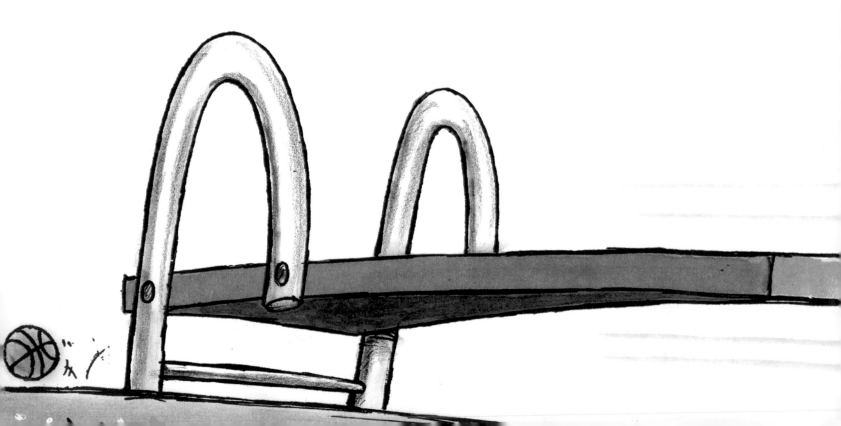

Play hide-and-seek?

¿Jugar al escondite?

28 . . .
29 . . .
30!

Ready or not, here I...

Listos, ¡allá...

. . . come.

. . . voy!

A movie?
¿Ir al cine?

Eesh.
¡Oh, oh!

WHISTLE?
¿SILBAR?

I guess a dragon doesn't make
a very good playmate after all.

Al fin y al cabo, quizás un dragón
no sea el mejor compañero de juegos.

You go home!
¡Tú, a casa!